D1695318

WHEN I SEE YOU IN MY DREAMS

Written by Ramiqa Hopewell, M.A., MNLC
Contribution by Ramiq a'King Hopewell
Edited by Deonna Augustine
Illustrated by Visoeale

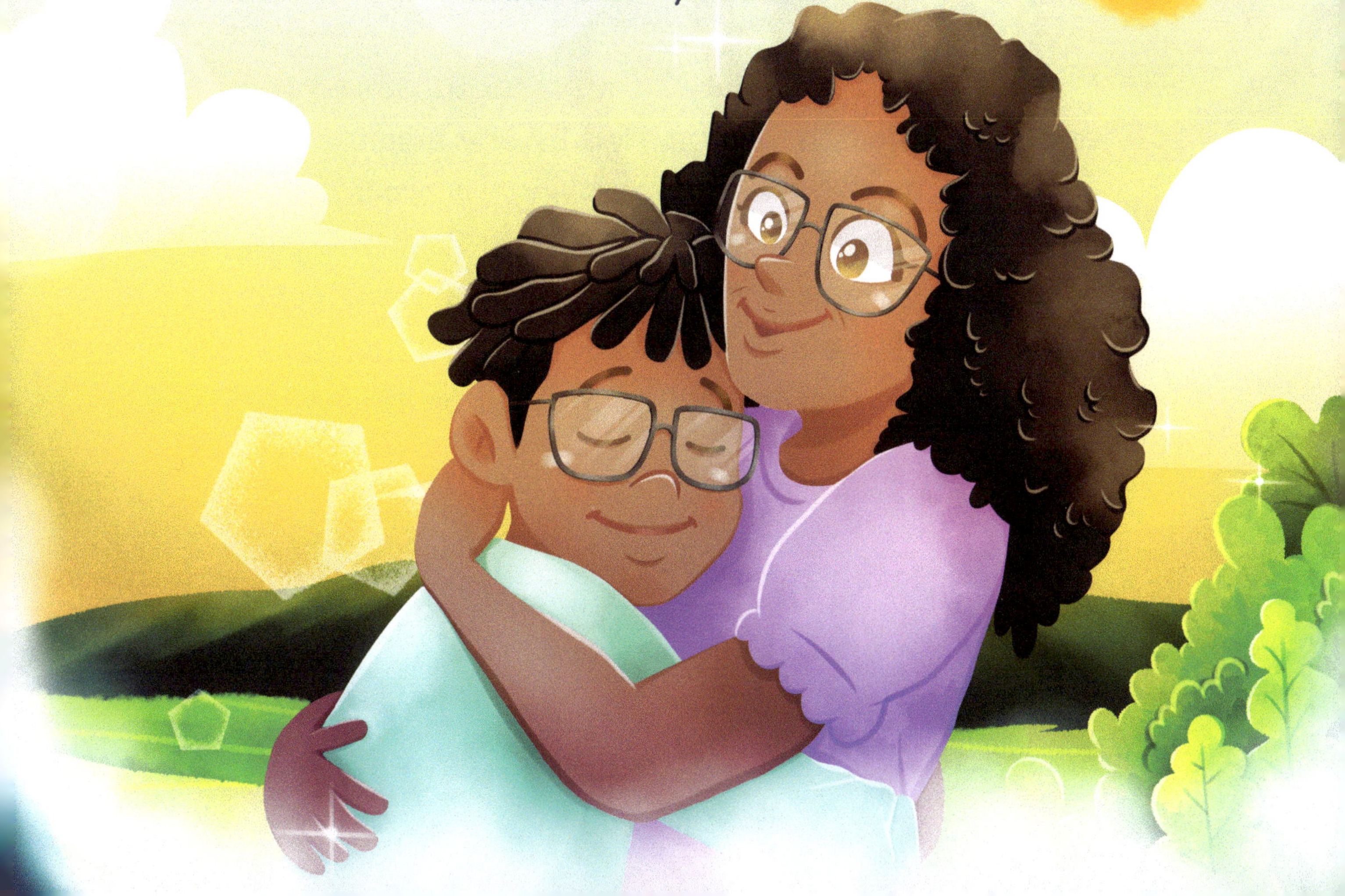

Copyright © 2021 by Ramiqa Hopewell

All Rights Reserved

No part of this book may be reproduced, stored in a retrieval system, or transmitted by any means, electronic, mechanical, photocopying, recording, or otherwise, without written permission from the author or publisher. There is one exception. If anyone opposes the rights of the author, Ramiqa Hopewell, on her claim or accusation, charges will be pressed on the subject.

THIS BOOK BELONGS TO:

_____

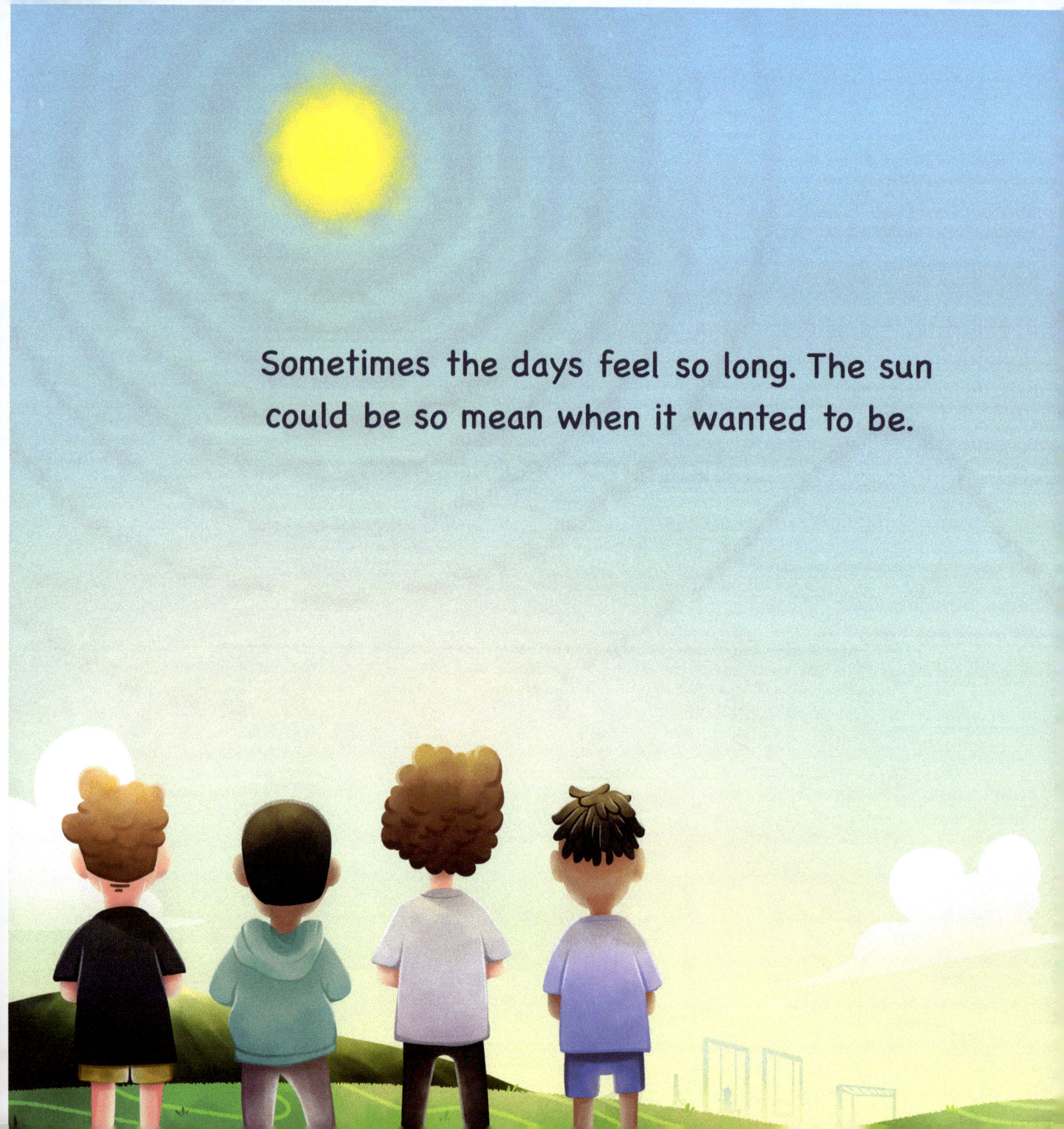

Sometimes the days feel so long. The sun could be so mean when it wanted to be.

I would sit and look at all of the kids playing in the park.

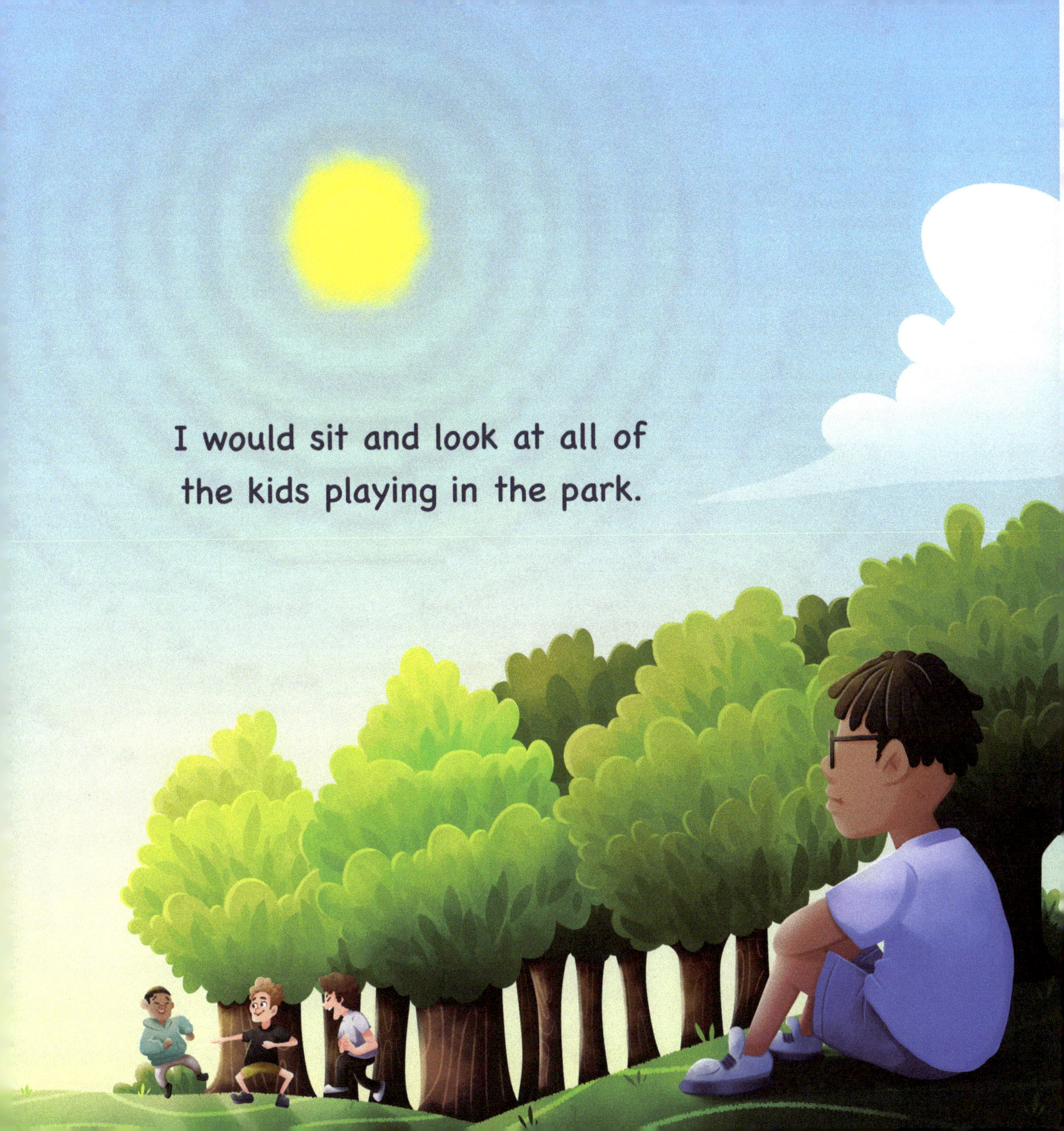

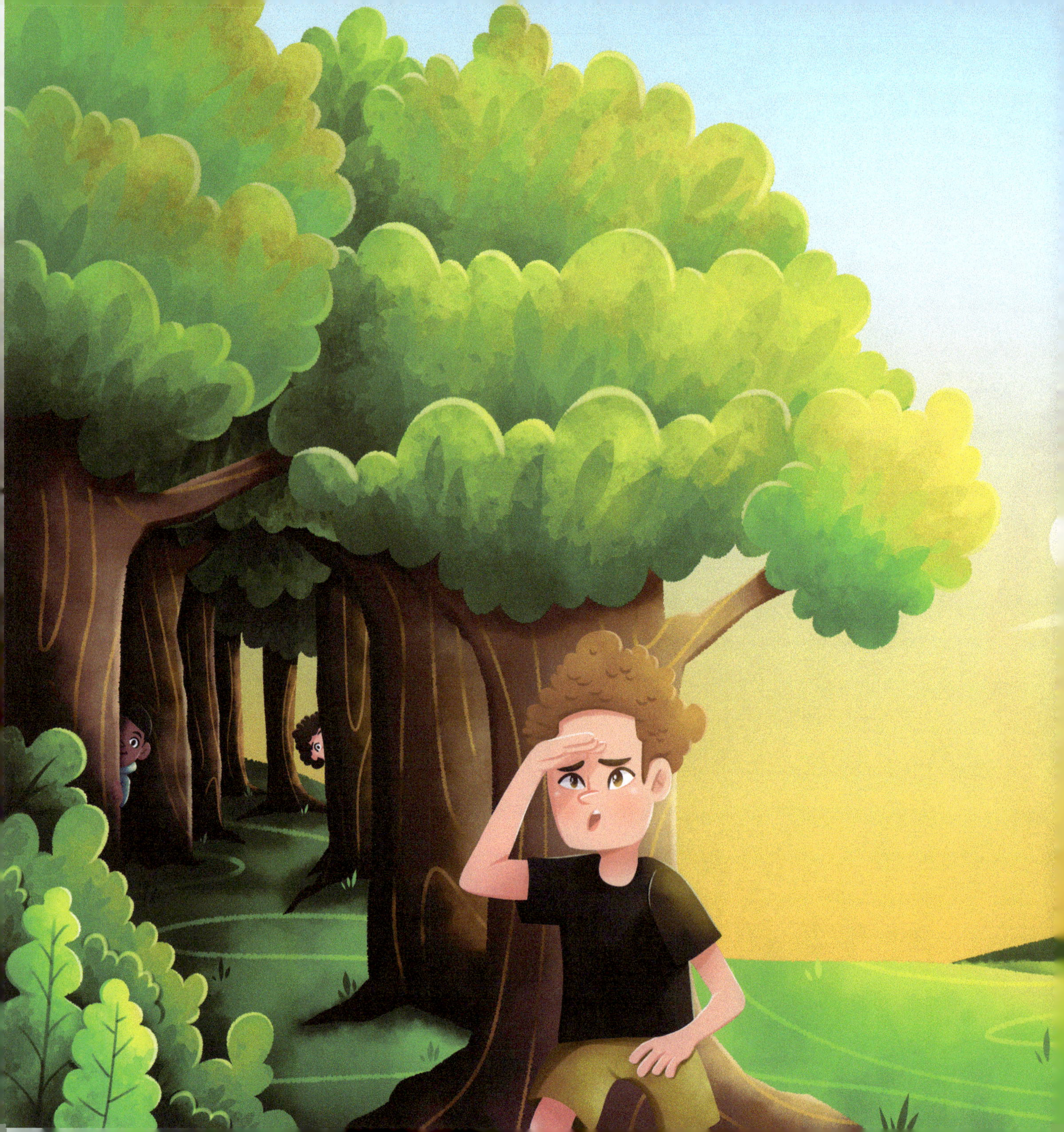

I remember how I used to enjoy playing hide and seek. I understood what the other kids felt, but the way they were enjoying themselves would never make the sun want to take a break.

It's been so long since I've been able to have fun like the other kids. But I could see night was coming soon!

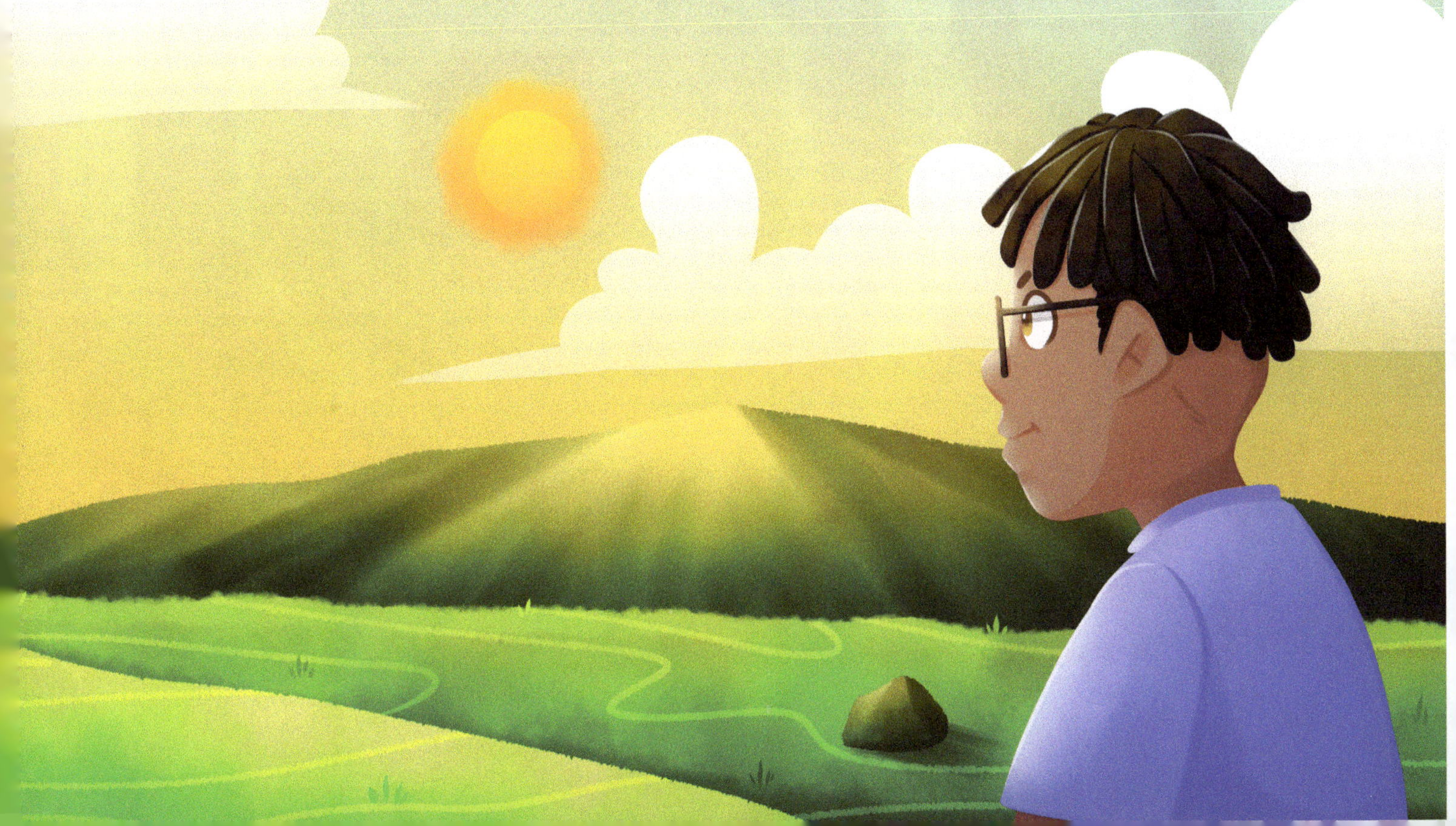

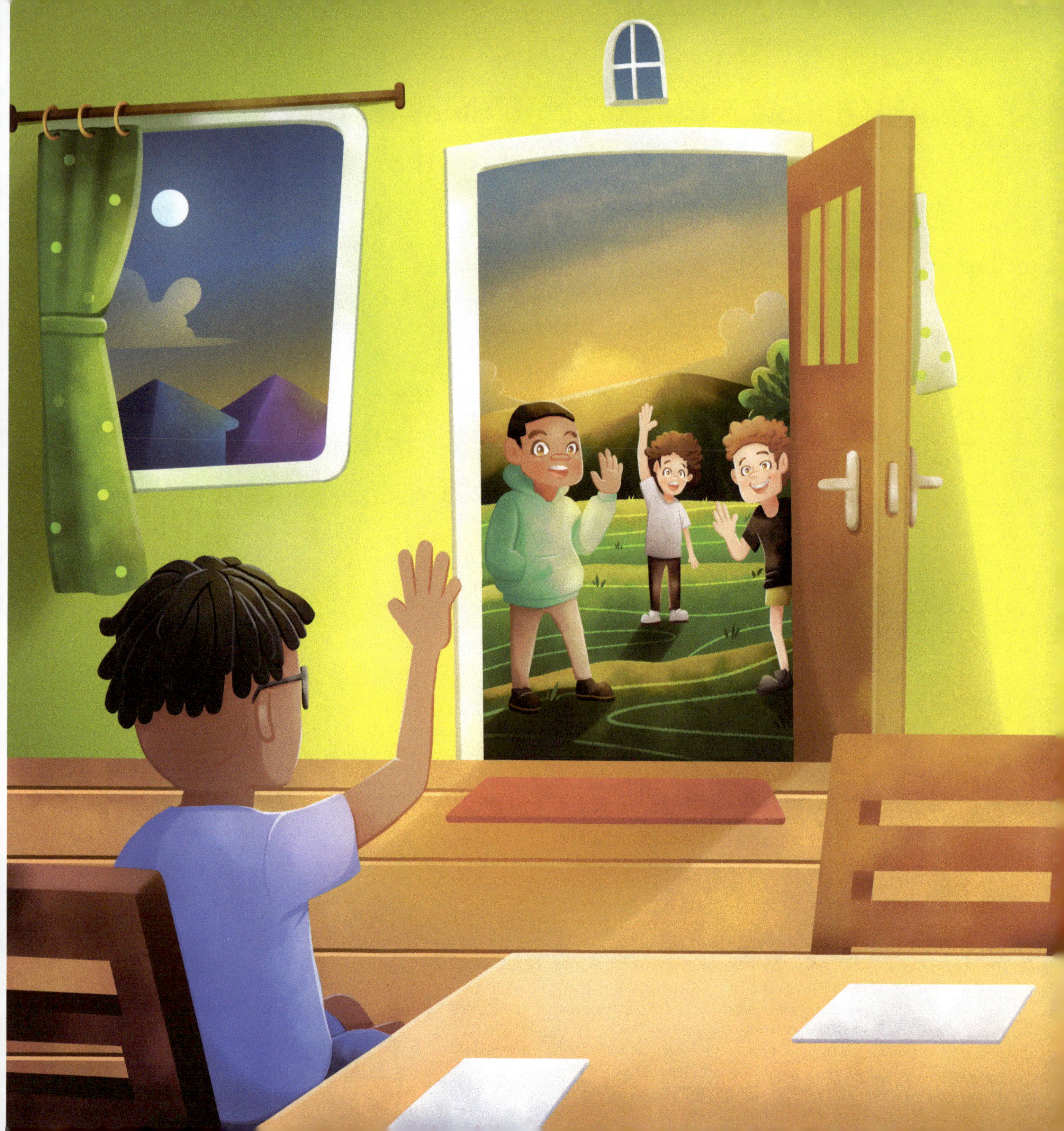

Grandma called me in the house to get ready for dinner. She always looked concerned when she saw me sitting alone.

I rushed to eat my pizza as fast as I could. I asked to be excused as soon as I finished my food.

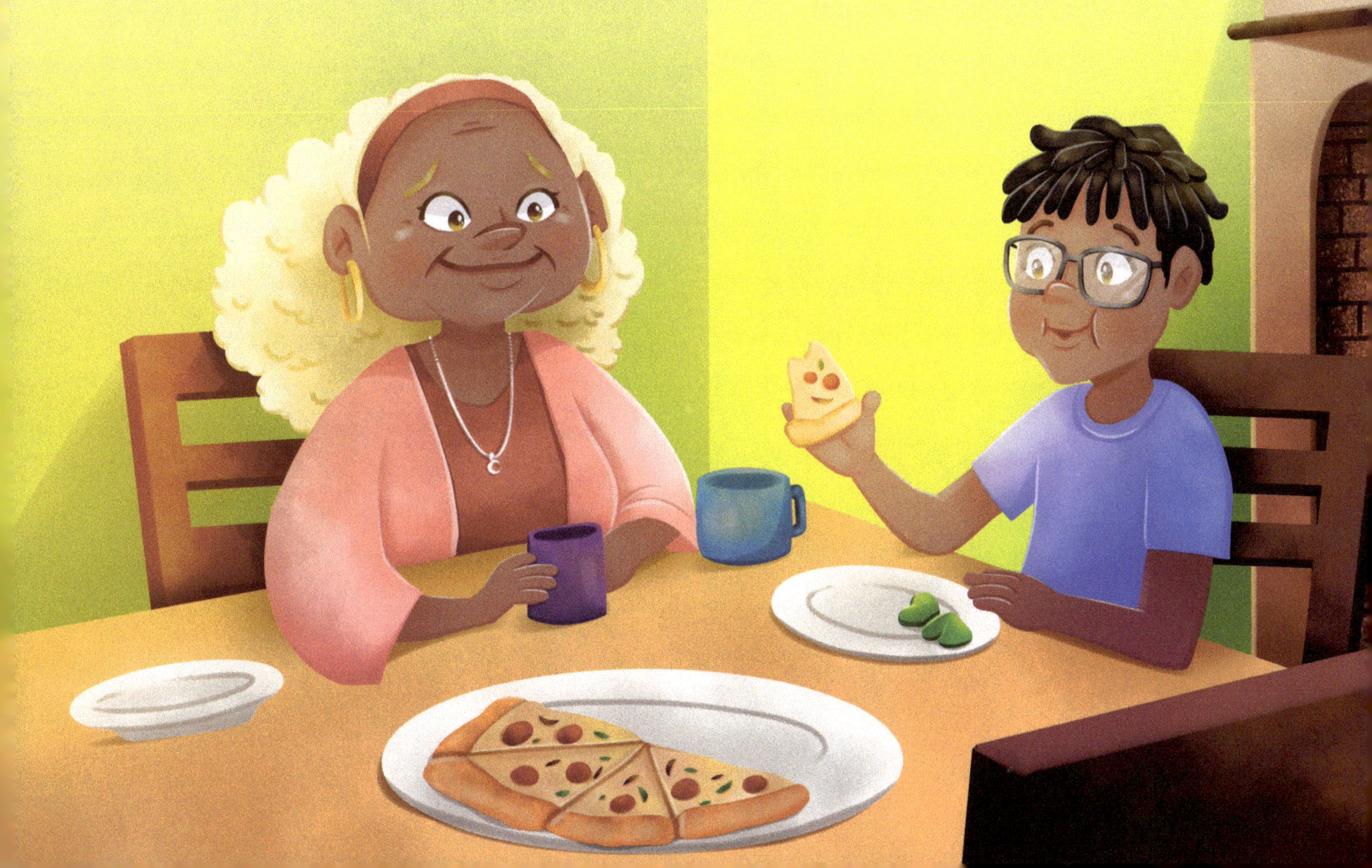

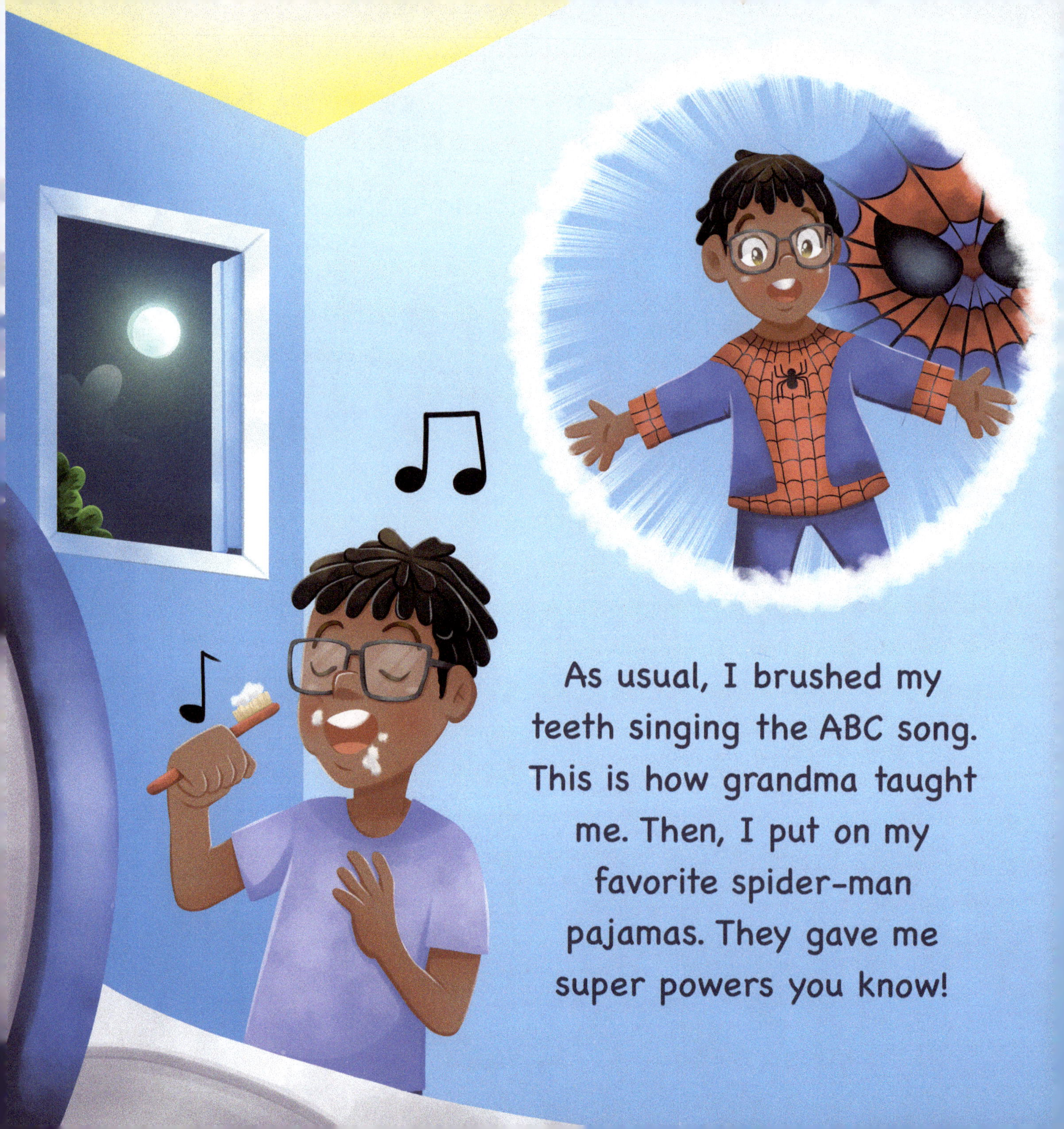

As usual, I brushed my teeth singing the ABC song. This is how grandma taught me. Then, I put on my favorite spider-man pajamas. They gave me super powers you know!

Grandma always came to tuck me in at night and say our good night prayers. As I finished, I closed my eyes really tight. The faster I went to sleep, the faster I got to see you in my dreams.

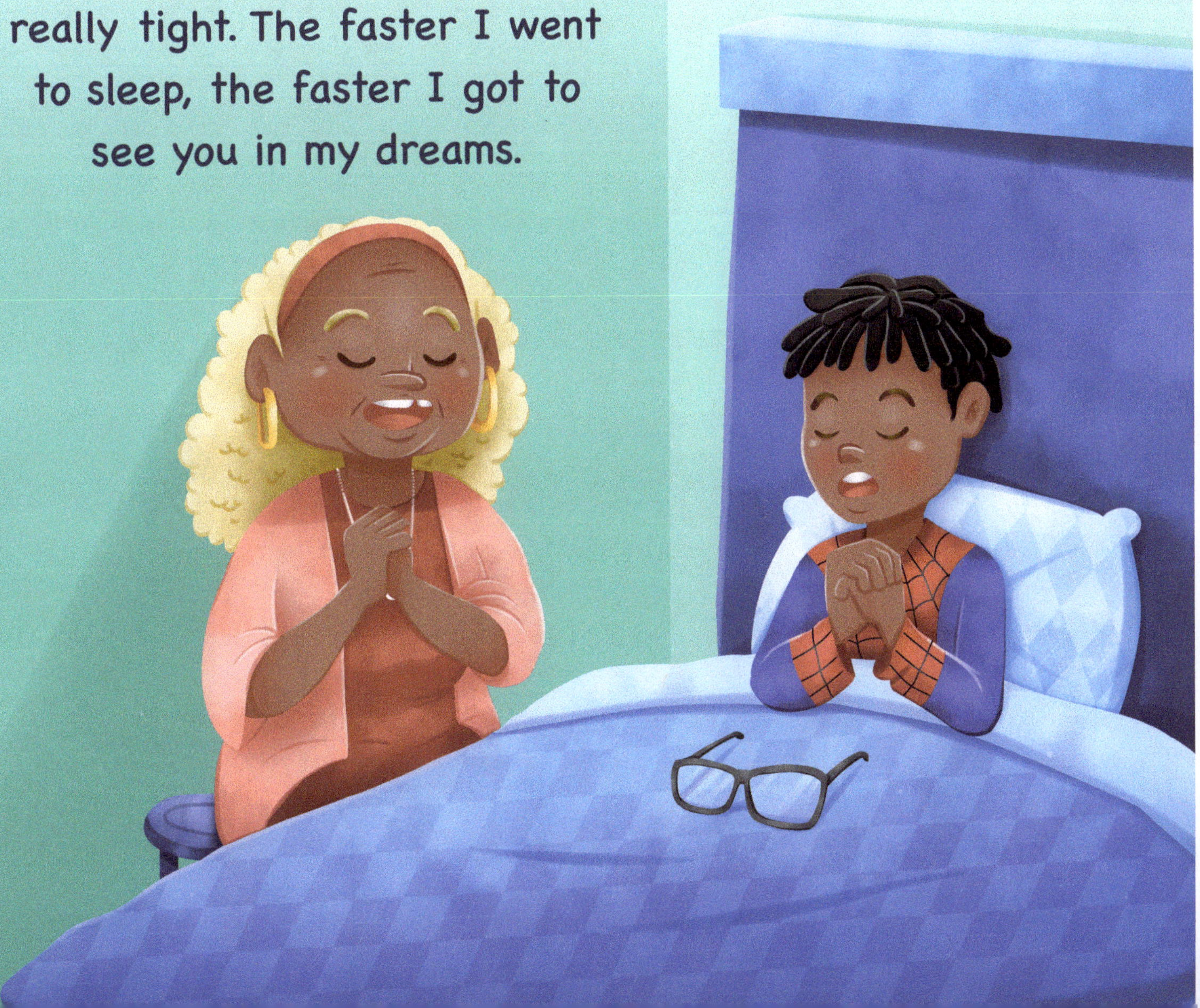

I know I'm asleep
when I see your face.
You would feel so
close to me.

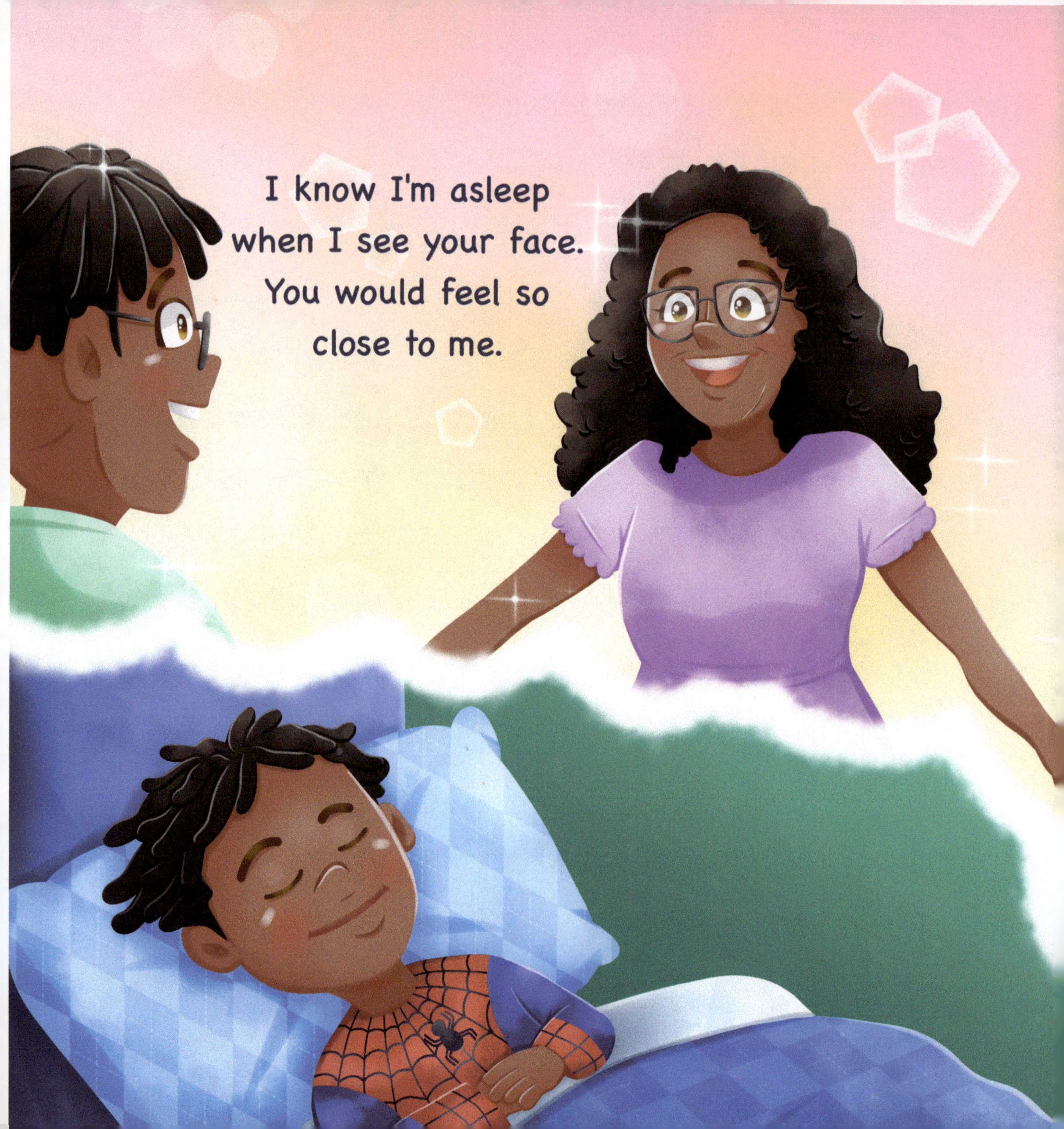

I could feel your hugs as you squeezed me so tight. I know I used to tell you it was hurting, but I was only playing.

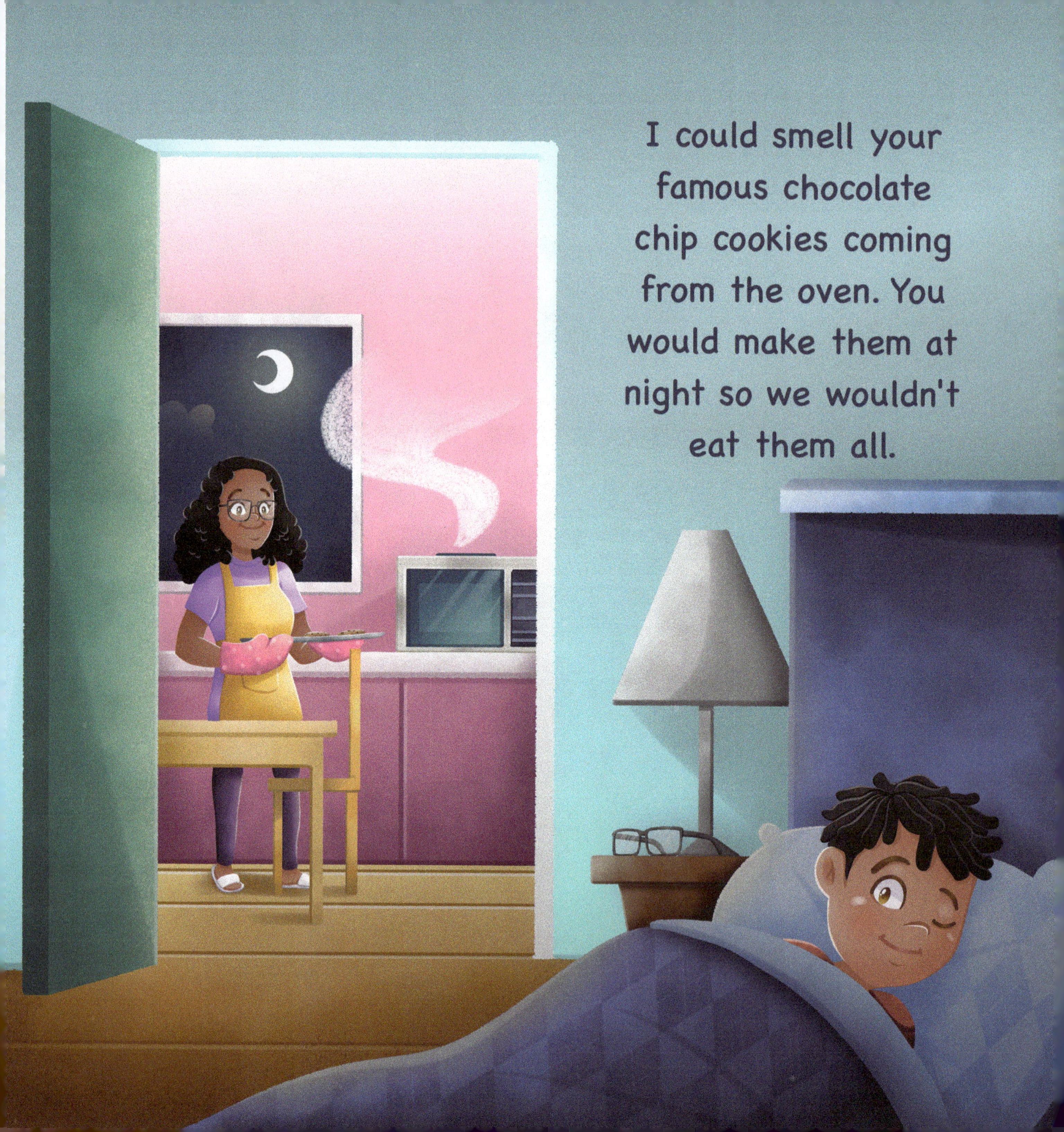

I could smell your famous chocolate chip cookies coming from the oven. You would make them at night so we wouldn't eat them all.

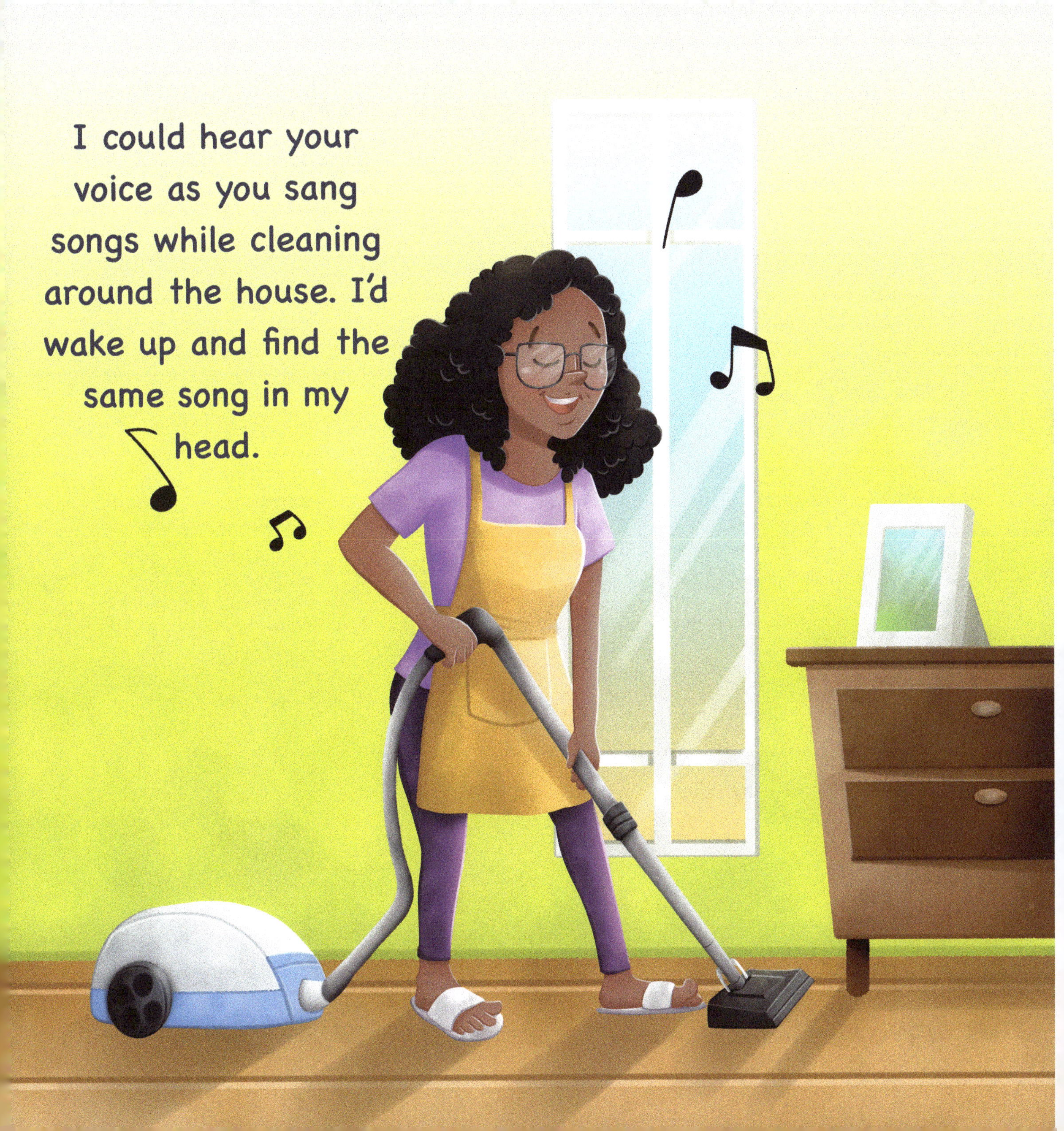

I could hear your voice as you sang songs while cleaning around the house. I'd wake up and find the same song in my head.

I could see how you cared for your plants in the garden. In the mornings, you would smile at the leaves that grew.

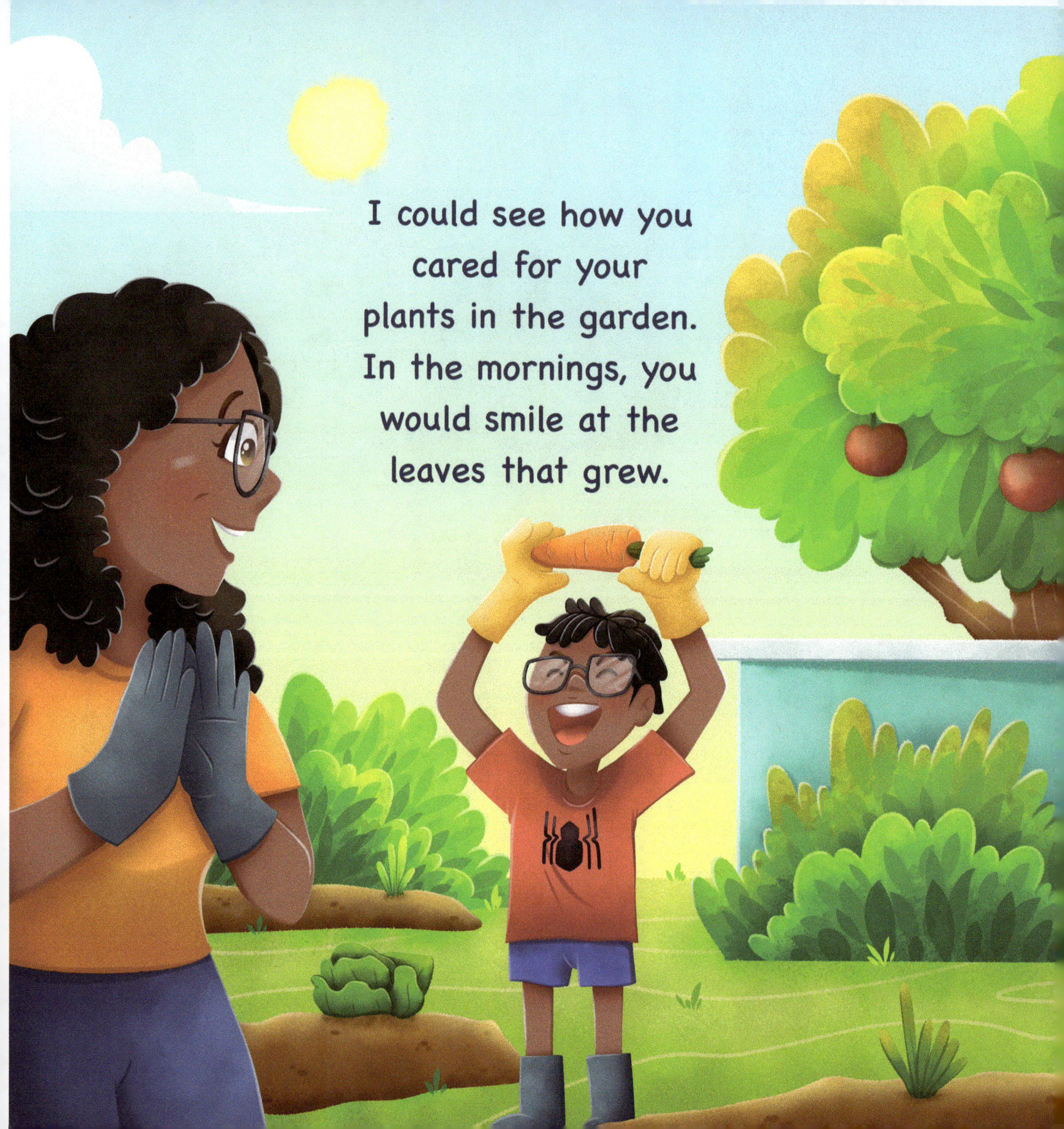

Can you believe my stomach actually growled in my dreams? I can still taste your Sunday afternoon cooking. Spaghetti was always my favorite.

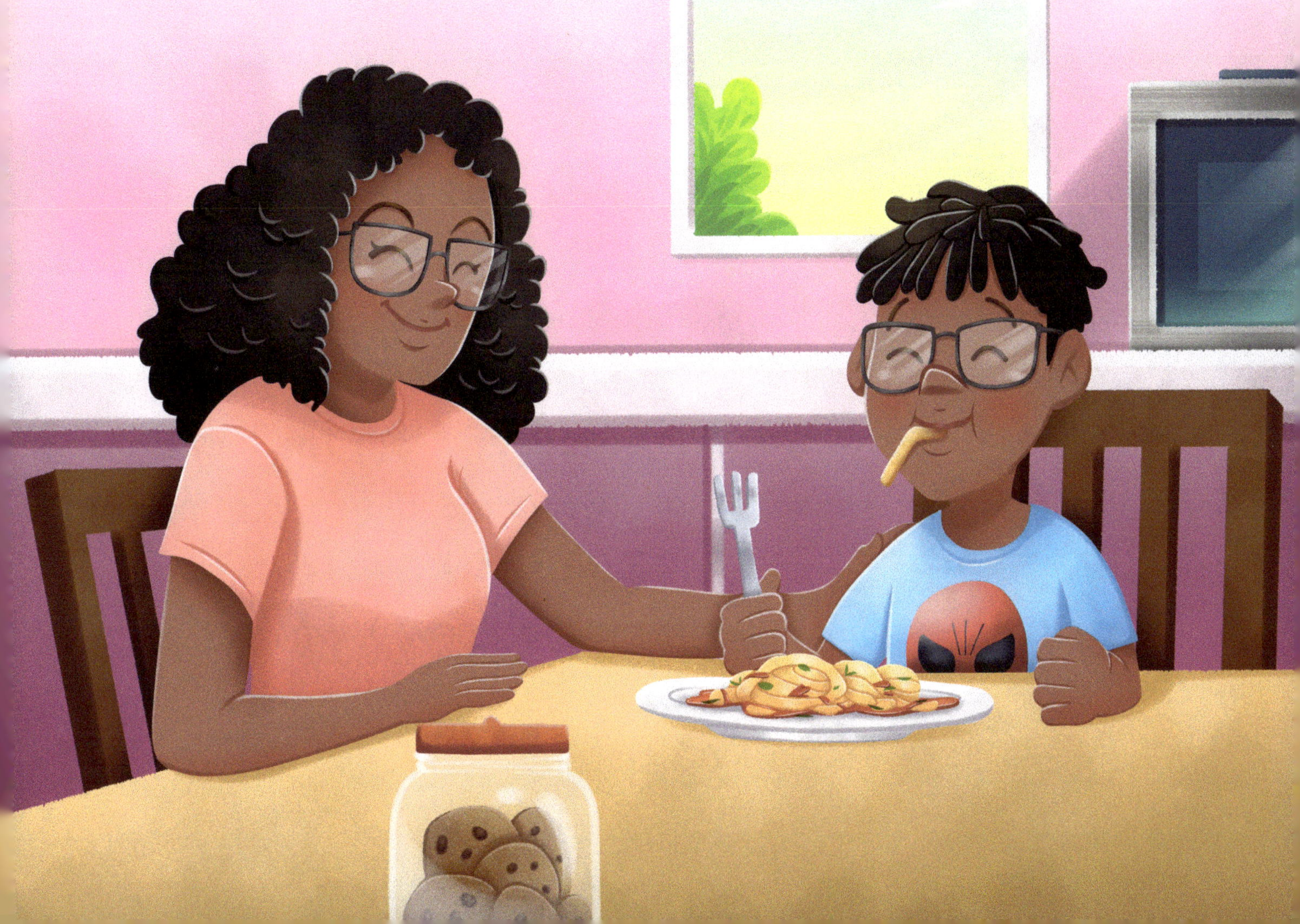

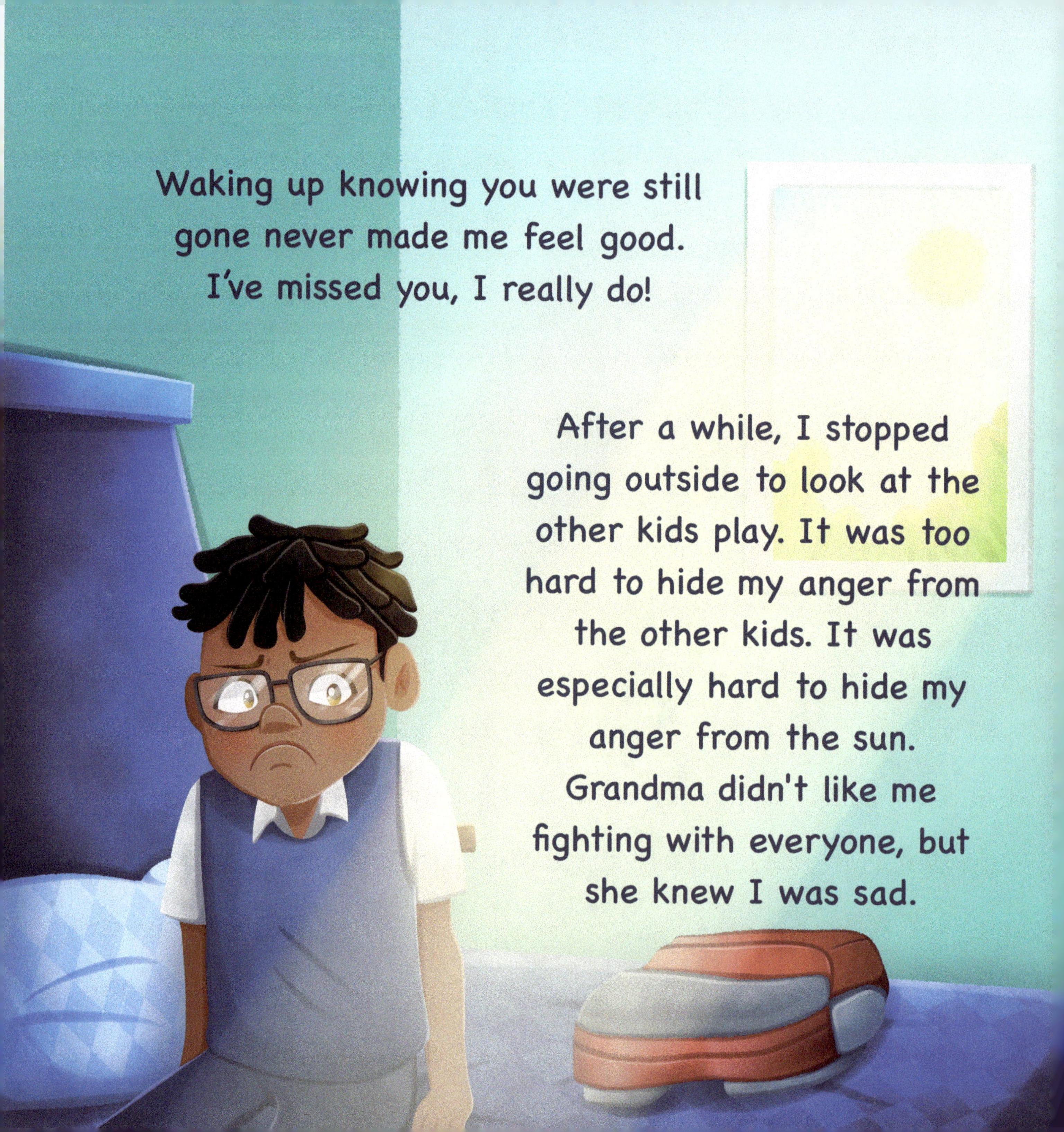

Waking up knowing you were still gone never made me feel good. I've missed you, I really do!

After a while, I stopped going outside to look at the other kids play. It was too hard to hide my anger from the other kids. It was especially hard to hide my anger from the sun. Grandma didn't like me fighting with everyone, but she knew I was sad.

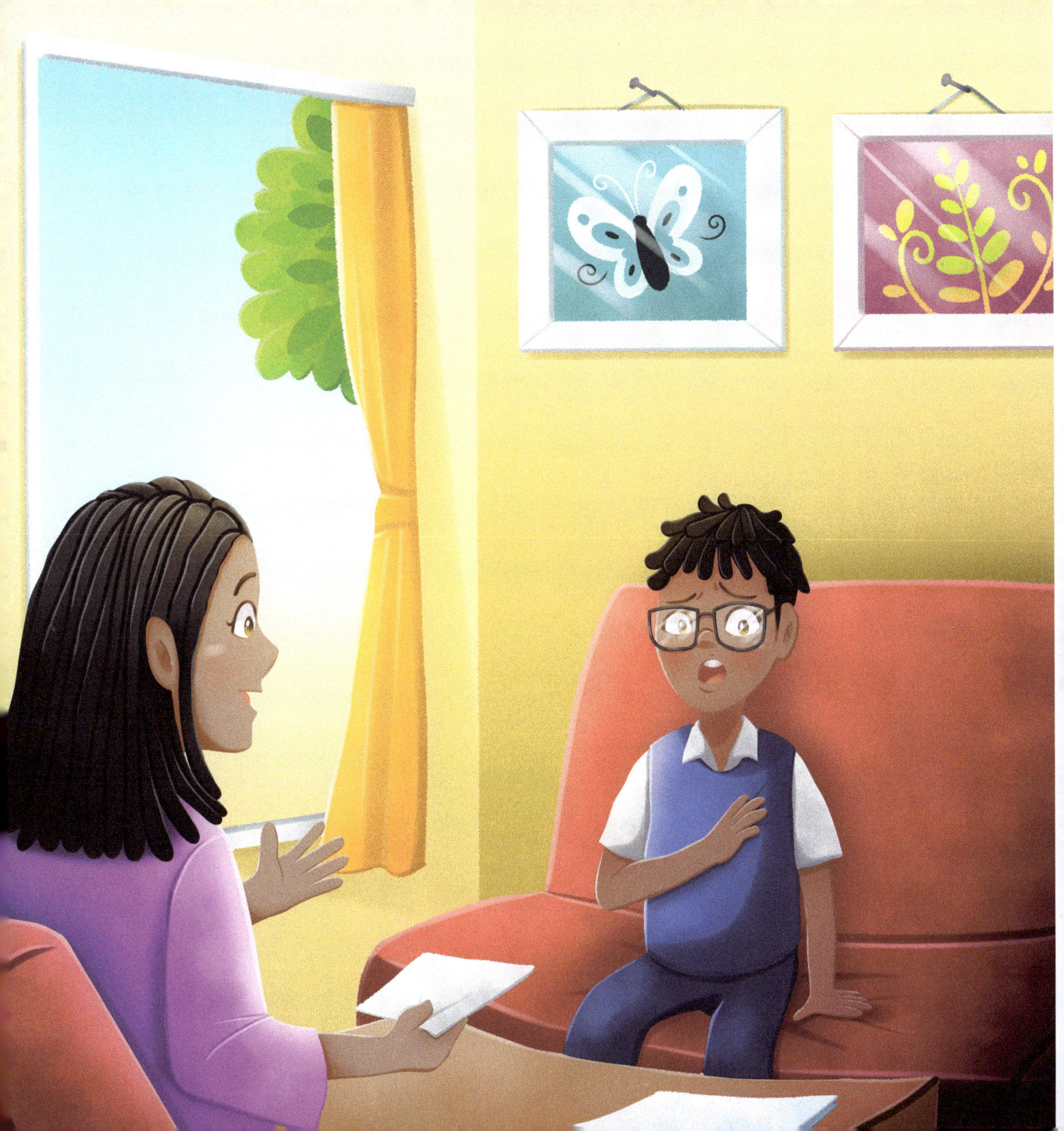

I was glad Grandma made arrangements for me to talk to a counselor at school. My counselor was really nice and helpful. My counselor helped me understand my feelings and taught me how the sun was not my enemy. In fact, the sun was my friend.

She said the sun also gave me time to feel your love during the day. She taught me that my eyes could be open and I still feel you through the sun's rays.

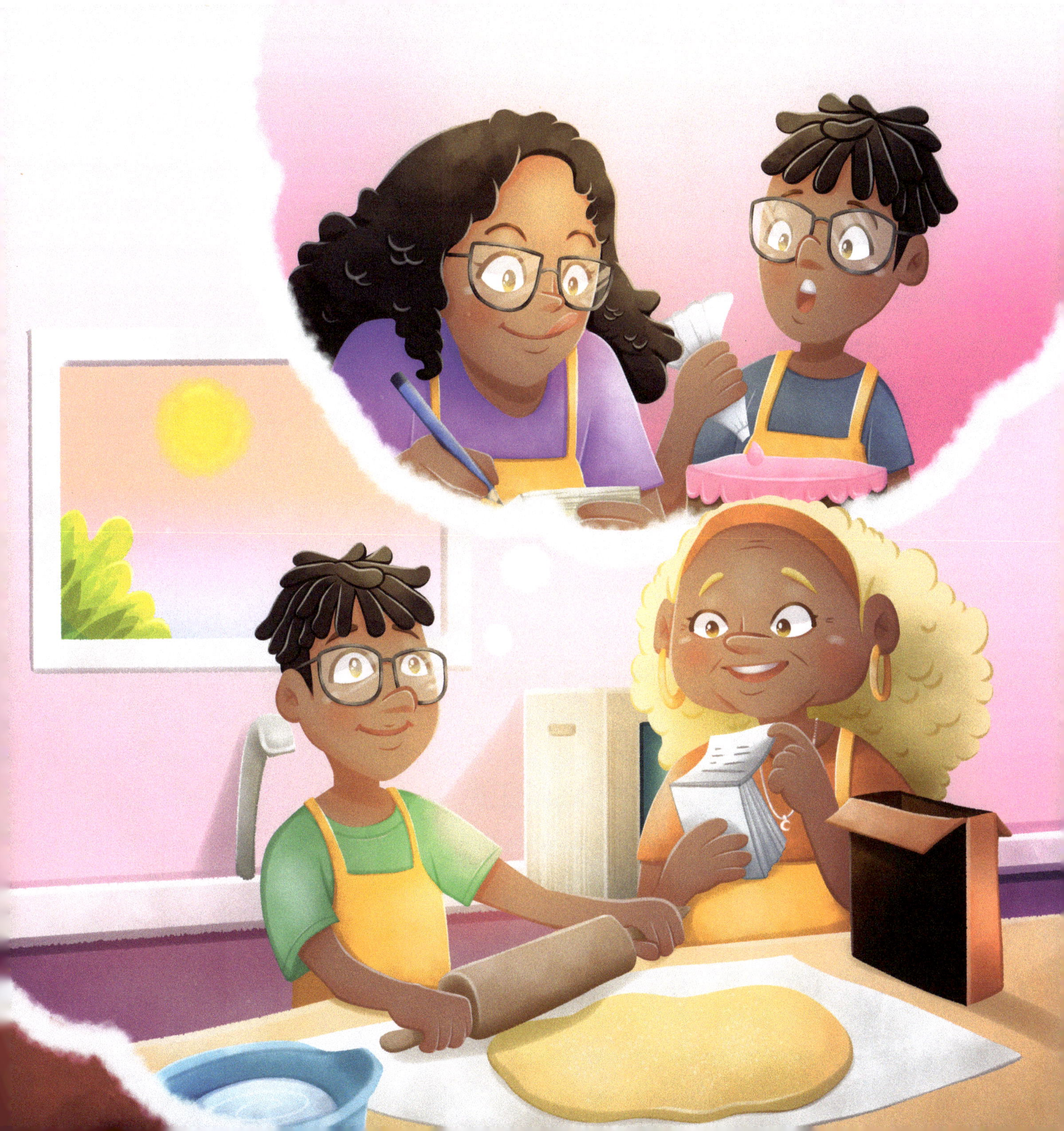

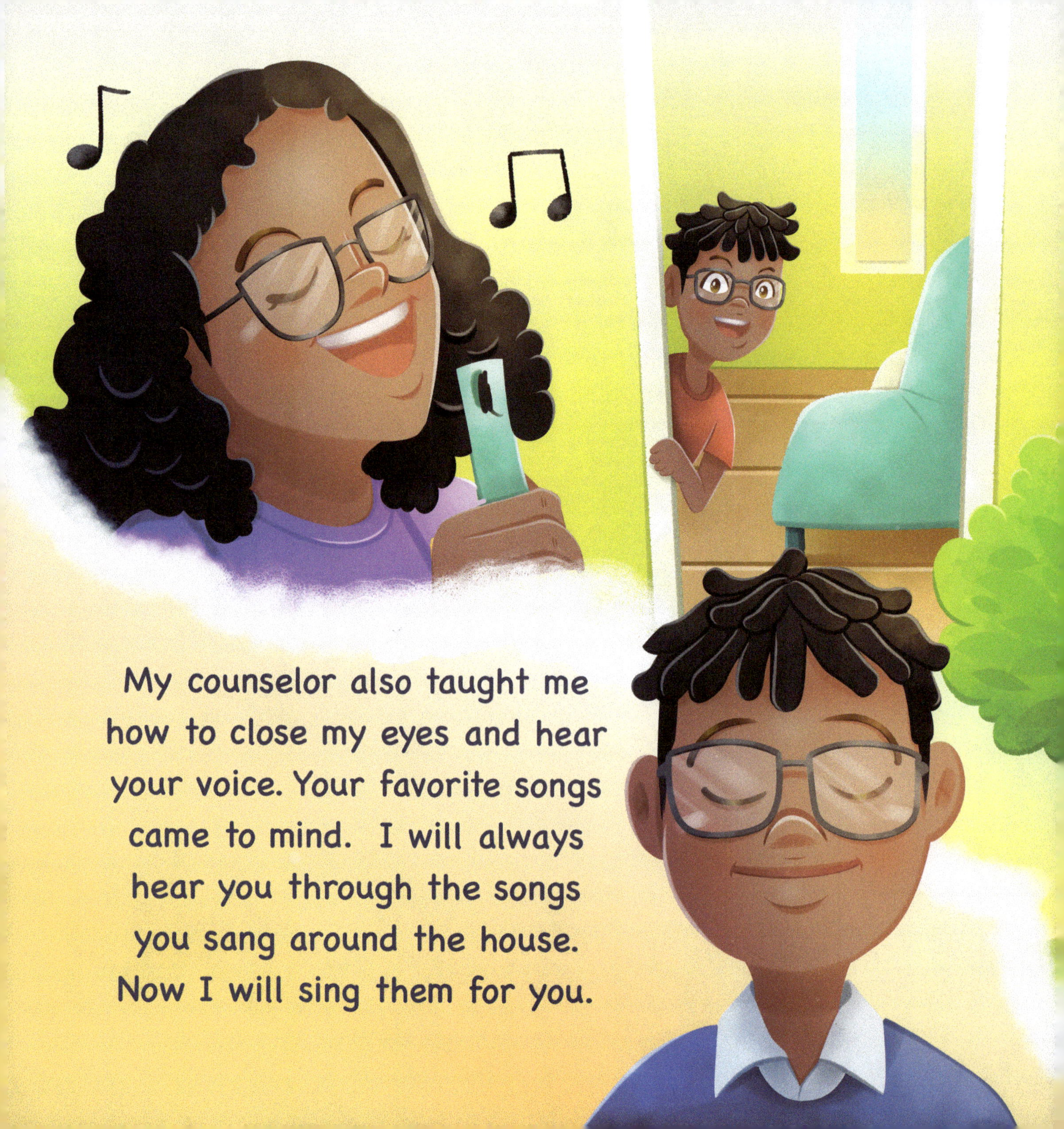

My counselor also taught me how to close my eyes and hear your voice. Your favorite songs came to mind. I will always hear you through the songs you sang around the house. Now I will sing them for you.

My counselor asked me about how the sun helped your garden. Once I thought about it, I remembered how the sun helped the plants grow! I will remember you through working in the garden with grandma.

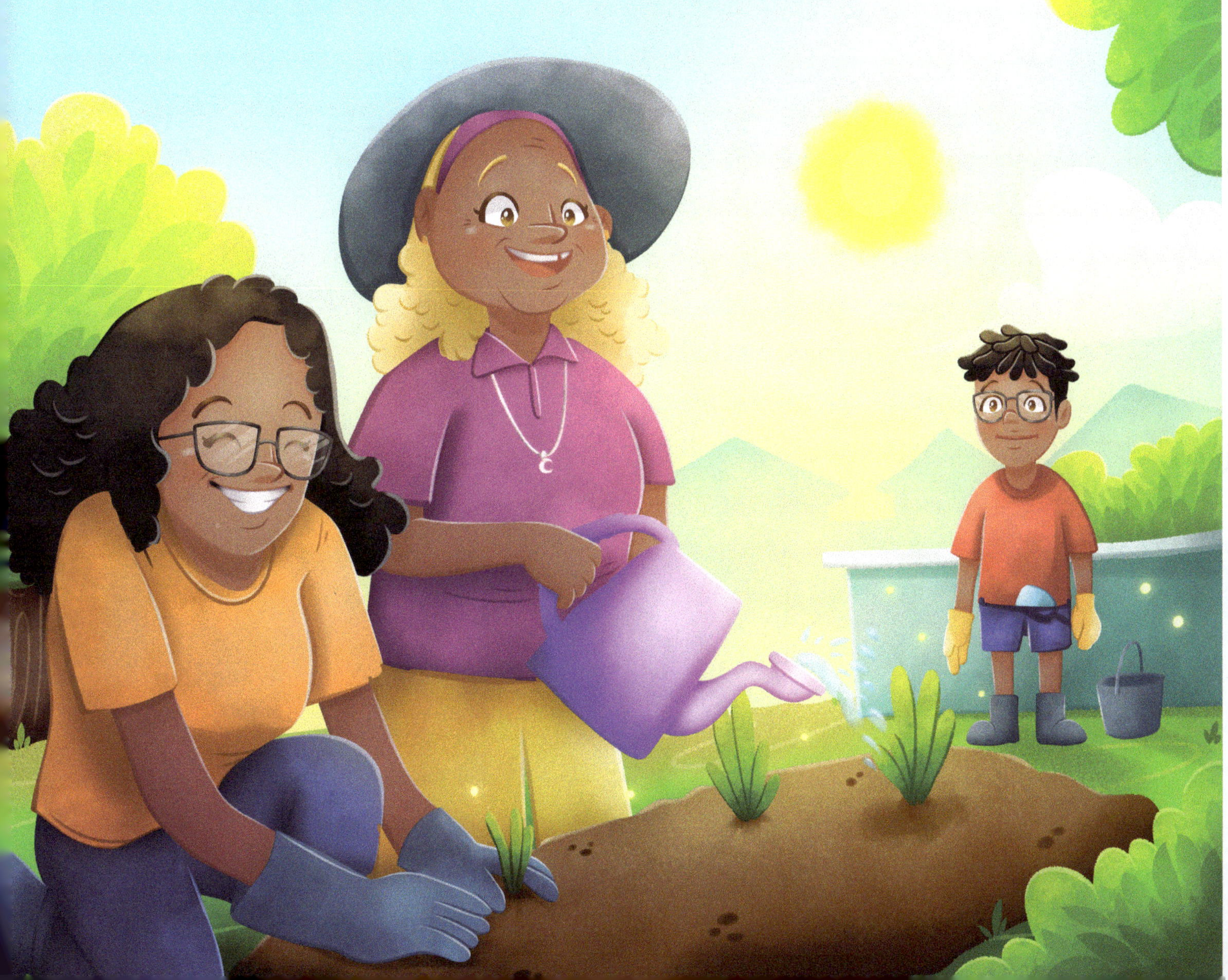

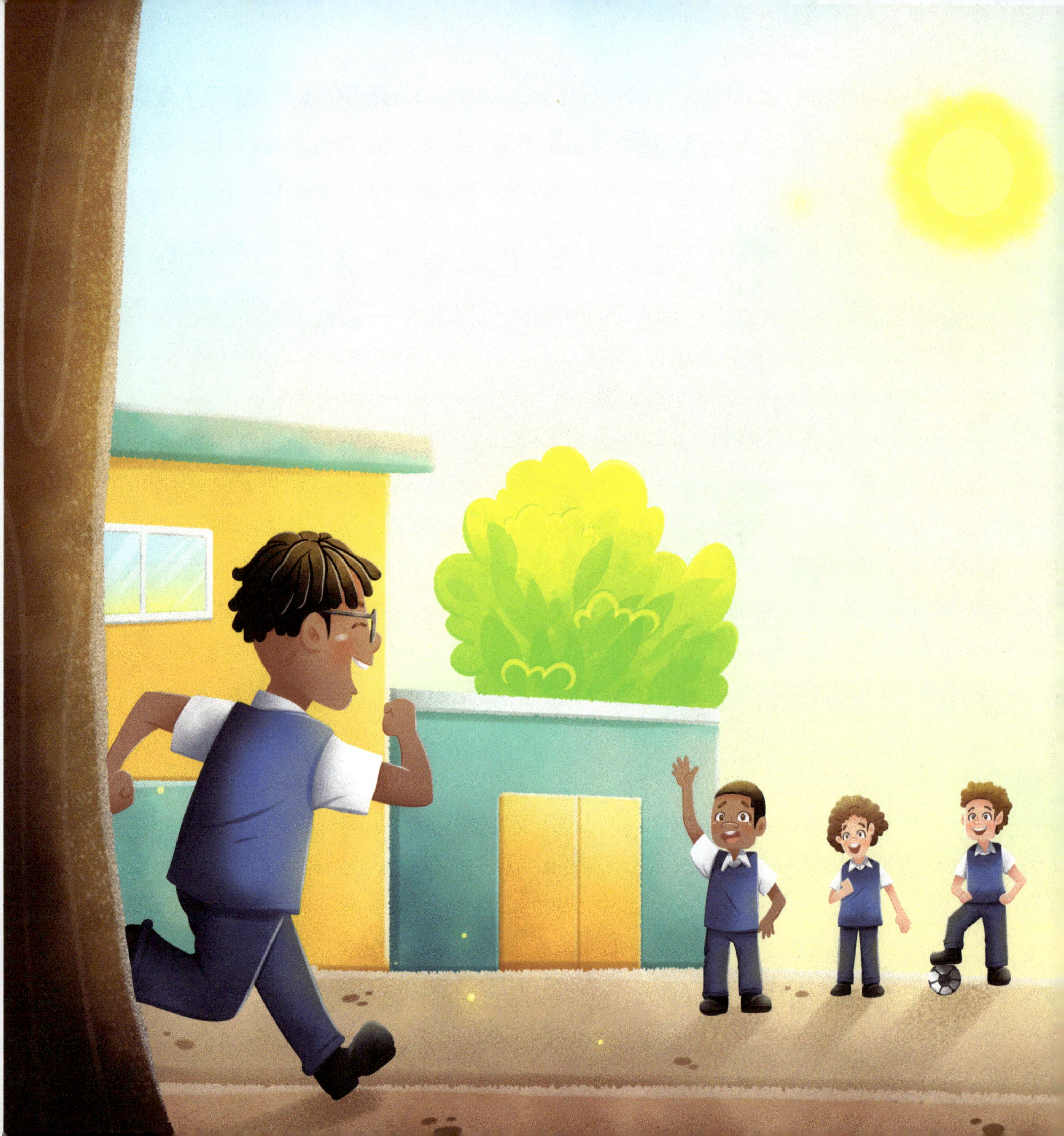

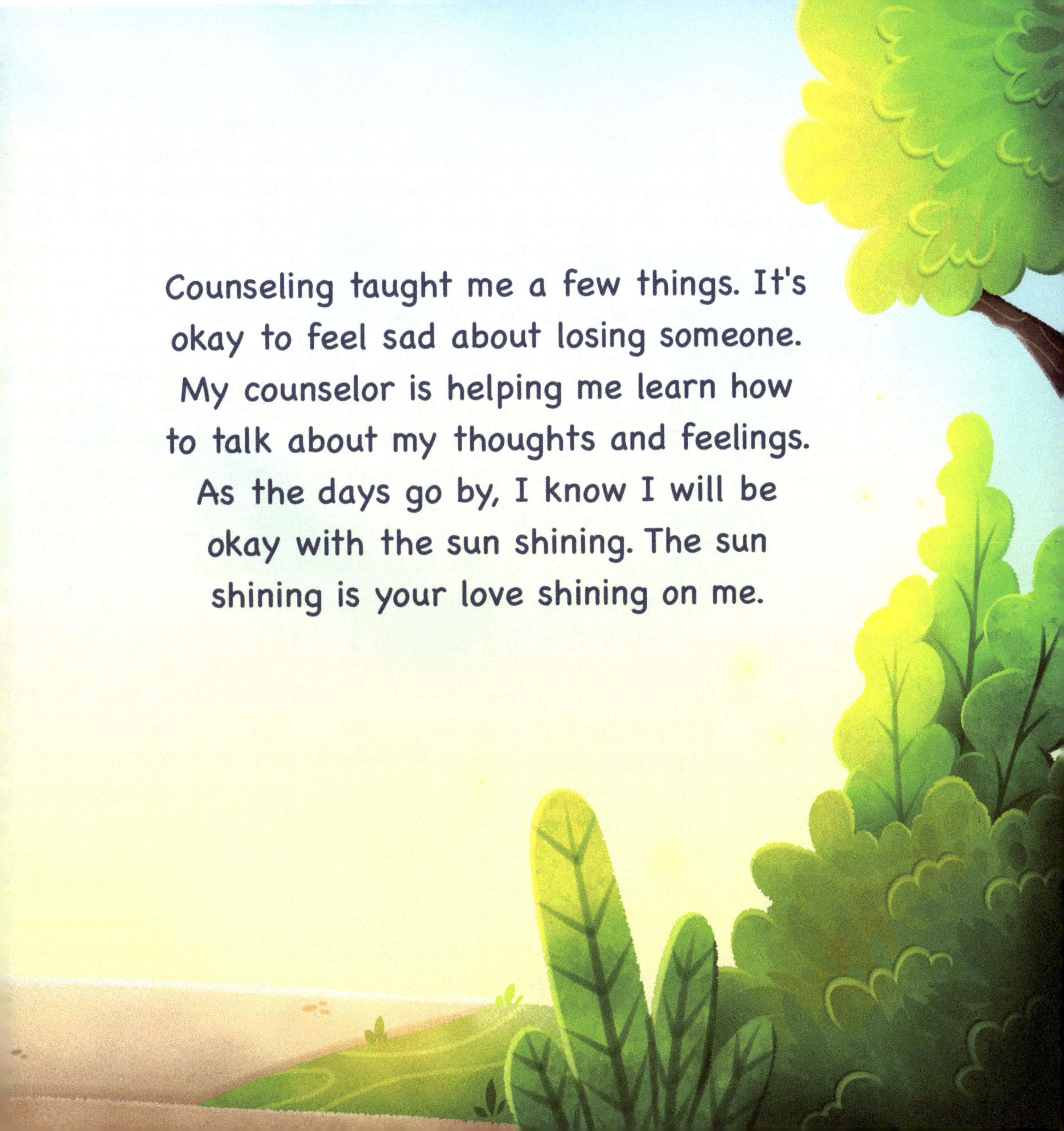

Counseling taught me a few things. It's okay to feel sad about losing someone. My counselor is helping me learn how to talk about my thoughts and feelings. As the days go by, I know I will be okay with the sun shining. The sun shining is your love shining on me.

Reading Reflections

Losing someone in our lives can sometimes feel like a lifetime of grief. To a child, it can feel like the biggest weight that has ever been carried. Children can have outburst of sadness all the while having moments of enjoying their daily activities. This book gives children a good introduction to counseling. Processing your thoughts and feelings with a counselor can be a positive way towards healing. These moments can come with symptoms of depression, anxiety, anger, isolation, and many other feelings. Below are some discussion questions that will help the reader understand and see how to relate to the character in this book.

1. What is the story about?
2. Is the boy in the story happy or sad?
3. Why do you think the character did not like the sun?
4. Tell me about a time you lost someone?
5. How do you think his grandmother can help him with feeling better?

6. What does grief mean to you?

7. How did you feel when you lost someone?

8. How long does it take to heal from losing a loved one?

9. What is a counselor?

10. Talk about your experience with counseling.

11. What questions do you have if you were able to speak with a counselor?

12. Talk about a special dream you can remember having.

13. Who can you talk to when you are feeling sad?

14. How do you remember your loved ones in a healthy way?

15. How can you help a friend deal with losing someone close?

16. What do you miss most about the person you lost?

17. If you could tell the person that you lost three things, what would it be?

18. What have you learned from this story?

19. What can you do to heal if you do not speak with a counselor?

20. Why would you blame yourself for losing someone ?

Go to **www.mentalnotelifecoach.com** to subscribe and download additional activities sheets for WHEN I SEE YOU IN MY DREAMS.

About The Author

Providing support for others exploring feelings and developing coping skills and tools has been a lifelong commitment for Ramiqa Hopewell. After completing undergrad at Florida agricultural and mechanical university, she went on to finish her masters in mental health counseling at Webster University. She has been a therapist since 2012.

As a therapist in Florida, Ramiqa now Support's children and adults through her practice Mental Note Life Coaching. She hopes to spark awareness and the importance of mental health and encouraging others to speak in honor of their feelings. Ramiqa is the best friend/wife to Cameron and the mother to two amazing boys, Ramiq and Rajon. The children's books written by Ramiqa are also in collaboration with her boys. Be sure to check out Ramiqa's first publishing, JAYA'S FEELING CRYSTAL.

You can learn more about Ramiqa's work and access therapeutic resources at her website:
www.mentalnotelifecoach.com

CPSIA information can be obtained
at www.ICGtesting.com
Printed in the USA
BVHW091001150421
605032BV00006B/662

9 781667 178325